Every year, more than a million wildebeest risk their lives. They walk 1,000 miles in long lines. The lines can be 25 miles long. On the migration, they face many dangers.

Ferocious predators hunt them. Lions and cheetahs lay in wait. If a wildebeest looks weak or slow, they attack.

Even young calves migrate. Some are only a few weeks old. They can get separated from their mothers. They can starve. Or they become easy prey for big cats.

On their route, there are wide rivers. The rivers have steep banks. They also have predators. It can be crowded. Wildebeest can accidentally fall or get trampled. When they reach the water, crocodiles wait. They hide underwater. They **man**euver to fallen wildebeest for an easy meal.

1

A river bank is the land along a river. River banks can be steep and dangerous.

Thousands of wildebeest die during migration. But they still make the journey every year. What are they looking for?

Chasing the Rains

Wildebeest live on grasslands and in woodlands in Africa. Wildebeest are herbivores. They are like zebras and gazelles. They only eat plants.

Plants need a lot of water to grow. So wildebeest go where it rains. Without rain, wildebeest don't have enough food to eat or water to drink.

Many wildebeest live in the Serengeti-Mara ecosystem. That's in eastern Africa. In this ecosystem, it does not rain all year.

There is a rainy season. It is from December to May. During this time, wildebeest live in the south. That's where it rains most. The grass and plants grow tall. Wildebeest find plenty of food and water there. And they have their babies.

It is a peaceful time for wildebeest. But it does not last. Soon they will start their annual migration.

Lake Victoria

Mara River

AUGUST–OCTOBER

Masai Mara National Reserve

Kenya

Northern Serengeti

JULY

Grumeti Game Reserve

Grumeti River

NOVEMBER–DECEMBER

APRIL–JUNE

Mbalageti River

Tanzania

Serengeti National Park

Lake Ndutu

Ngorongoro Conservation Area

JANUARY–MARCH

Maswa Game Reserve

Lake Eyasi

N
W   E
S

The Wild Beast

It has a long face, beard, and curved horns. It can look scary. That's how it got the name wildebeest, or "wild beast." But it is actually a peaceful animal.

It weighs up to 600 pounds. And it can be up to 8 feet in length.

It has a wide chest.

It is a quadruped. It walks on four feet. Its legs are very slim.

They're social animals. They form small herds.

Males use their horns to compete for territory.

They're noisy. They make explosive snorts and loud vocalizations.

6

An Endless Plain

In the Serengeti-Mara ecosystem, there are different habitats. The most common is savanna. This is how the area got its name. "Serengeti" means "endless plain." The flat landscape seems to go on forever.

Wildebeest love the savanna. They graze on the open grassland nonstop. They're always on the move. They look for short, sweet grass. It is their favorite to eat.

There are other habitats there too. There are woodlands, rivers, and swamps. Many wild animals live there. There are elephants, giraffes, and ostriches. There are hippos and leopards. There are even monkeys and pythons.

People live there too. They are called the Maasai. The Maasai re**spect** nature. They have lived there for hundreds of years.

Humans and anim**al**s rely on the land.

Savanna without Wildebeest

Wildebeest rule the savanna. There are more of them than all other herbivores combined. There are so many of them. They have a big impact on the land.

How do we know?

A **disease** came to Africa in the 1880s. It infected cattle. It made them sick. The cattle spread it to other animals. It killed many wildebeest. The population was dangerously low. And the entire ecosystem changed for the worse.

Fewer trees grew. There were more fires. Many animals left the area. There were fewer big cats. There were fewer birds and fish.

The ecosystem suffered without them. It needs wildebeest.

Without wildebeest, the ecosystem suffered.

When the wildebeest population recovered, the ecosystem did too.

An Explosion of Life

Scientists **man**aged to create a medicine. It cured the disease. The wildebeest population exploded. Soon, there were more than a million! The population was back. It transformed the ecosystem.

This at**tract**ed lions, cheetahs, and hyenas. They fin**a**lly had enough prey. Wildebeest ate the grass. They kept it short. So there were fewer fires. And their droppings put **nutrients** back into the soil. This helped new plants to grow. There were more trees. Large birds and fish came back too.

The wildebeest support the entire ecosystem.

The Great Migration

The rainy season ends by June. The south dries up. The wildebeest need to find water. They migrate north.

They begin their long journey. But they are not alone. Thousands of zebras and gazelles go with them. Over two million wild animals migrate together. Some call it "The Great Migration." It is a **spect**acular sight.

Herds crossing the Mara River

Before they reach the north, they have to cross the Mara River. This is the most **perilous** part of the journey.

Lines of wildebeest wait their turn to cross. They must climb down a steep river bank. Big cats hunt for prey. Crocodiles wait in the murky water.

The river can be fat**al**. Many wildebeest never make it to the other side.

Waiting for Rain

After weeks of walking, the wildebeest finally reach the woodlands in the north. There are more permanent sources of water there. But there isn't much grass. The wildebeest miss the sweet grass of the south.

But they have to wait. They wait for the next rainy season to go back.

The herds stay in the north until November. That is when the rainy season starts again. And they can return to the more nutritious grasses in the southern plains.

Threats Facing the Herd

Today, the wildebeest population is healthy. There are still millions of them. But they face threats.

Habitat Loss

People are farming more. They are raising more livestock. They put up fences. They pave more roads for cars. There is less grazing land for wildebeest. And it is harder for wildebeest to roam and graze.

Drought

Rivers need rain. Without it, they dry up. Then wildebeest have to travel longer distances for food and water. They might not find enough food or water at all. Scientists expect more droughts in the future.

Illegal Hunting

Many people in the local villages are poor. They often hunt wildlife. They need meat to eat. Or they sell the animals to make money. That includes wildebeest.

If wildebeest disappear, their whole ecosystem will change. Humans, animals, and plants need them.

Our One Planet

There are many ways to help keep wildebeest healthy. We can help even if we do not live there. We can keep our planet healthy. That protects every animal's habitat. This includes the wildebeest.

Reduce Pollution

Try to use less energy. And create less trash. Every action helps. Turn off lights. Drink water from a reusable bottle. Recycle plastic, glass, and paper. Walk or ride your bike. It adds up. It helps keep our planet healthy.

Read, Read, Read

Learn about wildlife organizations. Many protect wildebeest and their habitat. Find out ways to support them. Keep reading. And share what you learn with people you know.

The wildebeest migration is a grand **spect**acle. Their ecosystem needs them to continue their epic migration year after year.

Glossary

Disease	An illness or sickness that hurts or kills living things.
Drought	When there is not enough rain. Water for plants, animals, and humans runs out.
Ecosystem	A specific area where plants, animals, the land, and the weather all work together.
Ferocious	Strong and fierce. Ferocious animals can be violent.
Nutrients	Something in food, water, or soil that helps animals or plants grow.
Perilous	Full of danger and risk.
Permanent	Lasting forever.
Savanna	An open grassland habitat with scattered trees.